This book is dedicated for everyone to perservere.

Listen to this book:
storyj.mp/auv6hwvty9d

"Bye, Mom and Dad," Reema says happily.

Reema is so excited when her parents drop her off at her grandparents' house for the weekend. She is excited to have fun on the hot, sunny weekend. She gets to play in the big backyard and park in the neighborhood.

Bye Mom and Dad

Reema sees a group of girls roller skating in the evening.

"Hi, are you new here?" Kelly asks.

"I am visiting my grandparents. Those are cool skates!" Reema responds.

"Yes, they are so fun, you can try them," Kelly says as she lets Reema try on her skates.

Reema tries them on but cannot stand on her own. Kelly and all her friends help Reema stand up. The girls hold onto Reema's hand and help her start walking. Slowly, Reema starts running on her roller skates.

"Yay, I am roller skating," Reema exclaims.

Reema gets the hang of roller skating but suddenly, she falls and hurts her knee.

"Reema! Are you okay?" Kelly shouts.

"No!" Reema cries.

Reema looks over and sees a little bruise on her knee. Grandpa comes running as he sees Reema fall.

"I am not roller skating ever again!" Reema says.

"It is okay, you are fine! I will hold your hand until you are ready and have enough practice," Grandpa says.

Grandpa immediately takes Reema inside and puts a band-aid over her knee.

Two days pass, and Reema has still not gone outside. Her knee healed, but she gave up on roller skating because she was afraid she might fall again. Reema was frightened to roller skate.

Reema's grandparents buy her a pair of roller skates.

"Look, Reema! We bought you a pair of roller skates to practice," Grandma says excitedly.

"No, I cannot roller skate. I give up!" Reema says.

"If you do not practice, how will you get better, Reema? Look, your friends are here to help you," Grandpa explains to Reema.

Grandpa encourages Reema to get up and roller skate.

Reema practices for one hour around the neighborhood with her friends and Grandpa by her side.

Reema almost loses balance, but Grandpa catches her. Reema starts to lose hope, but Grandpa does not let her give up.

Reema practiced every day with Grandpa and fell a few times. Within a week of practice, Reema was roller skating all by herself.

You're doing great Reema!

"Reema, nothing is easy! It becomes easy only when we practice for some time." Grandpa explains.

"Wow! I feel like a pro. Practice makes perfect!" Reema cheers.

Reema, nothing is easy. It becomes easy only when we practice.

Reema learned that practice is required to master a skill.

Glossary

Bruise- An injury

Encourage- To give support

Heal- To get better

Neighborhood- Group of people living together in a town

Require- To need

Skill- The ability to do something well

This book is dedicated to everyone facing a challenge. Never give up!

Keep trying until you get better. Giving up is not the answer, and failure will encourage us to get up and try again.

Practice makes perfect!

ABOUT THE AUTHOR

Harpreet Kaur is a creator who enjoys using her imagination to make stories for children. Harpreet encourages all to be positive and try their best always!